Secret Signs

ALONG THE UNDERGROUND RAILROAD

Anita Riggio

BOYDS MILLS PRESS

NOTE: The words communicated in sign language in this book are indicated by small capital letters, in accordance with American Sign Language linguistics.

Publisher Cataloging-in-Publication Data
Riggio, Anita.
    Secret signs : along the underground railroad / by Anita Riggio.—1st ed.
[32]p. : col. ill. ; cm.
Summary : A deaf child helps pass information along the underground railroad using his paintbrush and a panoramic egg.
ISBN 1-56397-555-6
1. Underground railroad—Fiction—Juvenile literature. 2. Deaf—Fiction—Juvenile literature.
[1. Underground railroad—Fiction. 2. Deaf—Fiction.]
I. Title.
    [E]—dc20   1997 AC CIP
Library of Congress Catalog Card Number 96-80777

Published by Caroline House
Boyds Mills Press, Inc.
A Highlights Company
815 Church Street
Honesdale, Pennsylvania 18431
Printed in Mexico

First Edition, 1997
Book designed by Amy Drinker, Aster Designs
The text of this book is set in 16-point Caslon 540.
The illustrations are done in watercolor and gouache.
Copyright © 1997 by Anita Riggio

To Lois and Burt Albert,
for secrets shared and signs given

Acknowledgments

My deep appreciation goes to Judy Finestone, Librarian, Pennsylvania School for the Deaf, and
to Ivy Pittle Wallace, Gallaudet University Press, for their support, expertise, and enthusiasm.
For inspiration, my thanks go to Ashley White, David Smith, Kyle Hayes, and Susan Hayes.
Thanks to Karen Klockner and Amy Drinker for their patient help.
And to Roland, Cloe, and Lucas Axelson—my love.

Luke put down his brush. His hands painted pictures in the air. I DON'T UNDERSTAND WHY YOU HAVE TO GO. SOMETHING BAD COULD HAPPEN TO YOU.

Mama signed, SOMETIMES IT TAKES COURAGE TO DO WHAT NEEDS DOING.

Luke shook his head, NO, MAMA, PLEASE. IT'S TOO DANGEROUS!

But Mama's eyes remained calm and gentle. WE HAVE A PLAN. THIS AFTERNOON, WE'LL MEET OUR CONTACT AT THE GENERAL STORE. I WILL KNOW HER BY HER INDIGO SHAWL. SHE WILL KNOW ME BY THE SUGAR EGGS WE SELL. IT WILL BE ALL RIGHT. YOU'LL SEE.

But Luke knew that two days ago slave catchers had set the Richards' barn ablaze. The Richards had been hiding runaway slaves. The people escaped, but the barn had burned to the ground.

Mama told Luke, NOW PRICE'S FARM WILL BE THE NEW HIDING PLACE. IT'S MY JOB TO PASS THIS INFORMATION ALONG.

Mama's hands returned to her work. But as she smoothed a maple-sugar shell, Luke noticed her long fingers trembling a little. He looked away. The boy could not bear to think of his mother in danger.

Luke turned back to his brush, paints, and parchment. He had been painting for more than an hour, but it hardly seemed so.

Now he peeled up the parchment and placed it at one end of the shell. After Mama rimmed the bottom half with icing, she placed the other half-shell on top of the first, forming a delicate, sugar-spun cradle for Luke's painting: rolling green hills, a woman, a boy, and a dog by a shimmery stream. He handed the egg to Mama, who tilted it toward the light.

OUR FAMILY? Mama's hands asked.

YES, Luke answered, smiling. Somehow, painting it had eased his mind.

Suddenly their dog, Ellie, jumped to her feet and bounded to the door, barking. Luke felt the floorboards shudder. Someone was pounding on the door. Mama went to answer it.

As soon as Mama raised the latch, a man pushed past her. A woman was behind him. Mama glanced at Luke, whose eyes grew wide at the sight of the intruders' grim faces.

SLAVE CATCHERS! Luke signed.

The man spoke to Mama, his lips curling back from his teeth. Ellie's lips curled back too, but Mama hushed her.

Squaring her shoulders, Mama shook her head. "You'll not find any slaves here," she said, signing so Luke could understand.

The man crossed the room. He snatched a sugar egg from the box and peered into it. He glared at Luke. Then, swinging around, he spoke to Mama.

Once more Mama spoke and signed. "You have no right to keep us here. My son and I are expected to sell our novelties at the general store today. Folks would wonder if we were not there as promised."

With one swipe, the man grabbed both of Mama's hands and held them fast. His face was so close to hers that his breath blew a few strands of her hair. Luke could still lip-read some of the man's words—"hiding slaves. . . ."

There was a rumbling in Luke's chest and throat. "No!" he yelled.

Mama turned. Her dark eyes burned into his. *Be brave*—they told him.

Ellie went wild. The man batted at the dog. Ellie snapped at him, but Mama soothed her again.

Luke read Mama's words as she spoke with one hand on the dog and one hand at her side. "Let us bring our eggs . . . no harm. . . ."

For minutes, it seemed, the man glared at the dog and then at Luke. The man shoved the box of eggs across the table with one hand and grabbed the boy's collar with the other.

"I'll take the boy," he sneered.

Now it was Mama who cried out, "No!"

Luke shook loose. I'LL DELIVER THE MESSAGE! he signed.

Turning away from Mama, Luke snatched his brush, paints, and parchment and swept them into the egg box. The man's bony hand clamped Luke's shoulder, pushed him past Mama, Ellie, and the woman, out the door and onto the wagon. Luke looked back. The door slammed shut.

The boy's heart thudded—*be brave—be brave—be brave.*
As the wagon bumped along the rutted road, Luke's fingers searched the eggs for the tiny painting of Mama, Ellie, and him. There it was. The paper was still damp and soft. With a quick glance toward the old man, Luke pulled the painting from the shell, crumpled it, and let it drop to the ground.

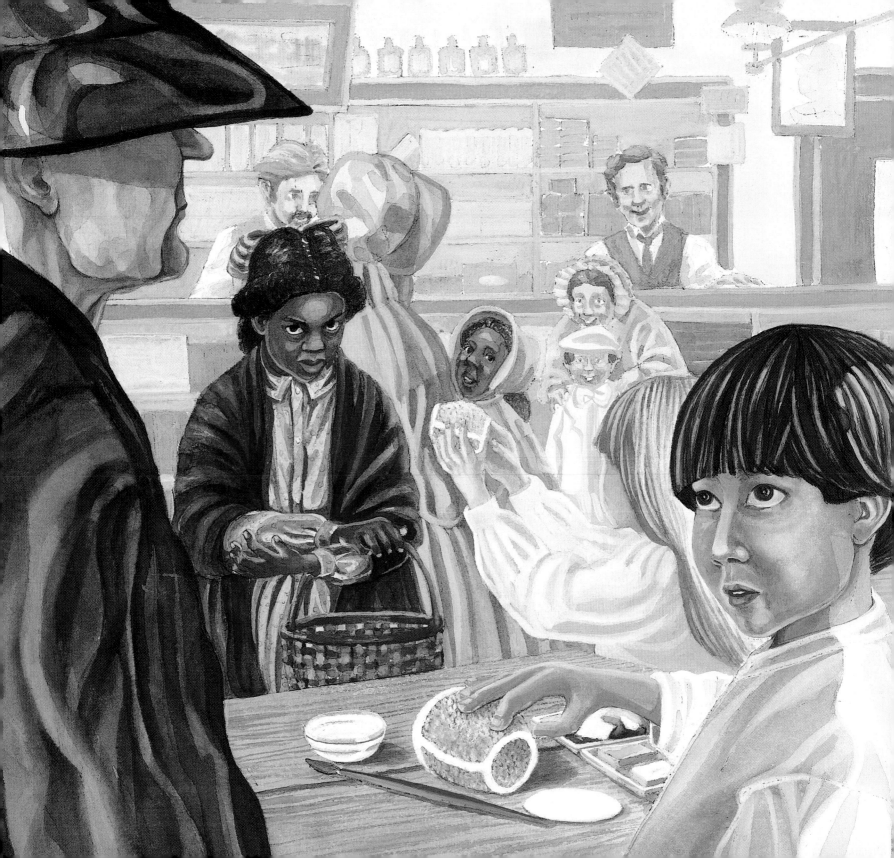

Inside the general store, Luke felt the man's eyes on him as customers scooped up the sugar eggs. Folks gathered around. In the crowd, Luke spotted a girl wearing an indigo shawl.

He laid out his brush, paints, and parchment. Beside them he set the empty sugar shell. His hand hovered over the egg for a moment, his fingers fluttering.

Luke peered at the man. Had he guessed Luke's plan? The boy dropped his gaze, his heart beating—*be calm—be calm—be calm. Sometimes it takes courage to do what needs doing.* He willed his fingers to be still.

With the crowd looking on, Luke took up his brush and felt the weight of it. He fixed his eyes on the parchment. Brush touch paint then paper: daub red, dash white, spot green, touch warm brown, swipe palest blue. . . .

When the boy finally looked up, he saw the crowd clapping approval at the miniature painting: broad sky and sweeping meadow, road, pond, and hills. In the distance, a red barn and a white house.

"Beautiful. . . ."

"Delicate. . . ."

Folks nodded and grinned.

Now Luke's feet sensed the signal he knew would come—the clomping of the man's heavy boots rippling the floorboards.

Be quick—be quick—be quick. The boy snatched the sugar shell and, wheeling around, thrust it into the old man's hand.

INTRODUCING…MY LOVELY ASSISTANT, mimed Luke. The crowd tittered. The girl in the indigo shawl giggled. The man reddened, glowering at Luke. But—*be brave—be brave*—the boy returned that glare with his own steady gaze. Glory! The man stood stock still, the fragile egg resting in his rough hand.

Now all eyes were watching, and Luke hardly dared to breathe. With one steady finger, he pushed the tiny, damp painting into the brittle shell.

The crowd clapped.

"Amazing. . . ."

"Wonderful. . . ."

Beaming, Luke took the egg from the man and displayed it. Then he bowed deeply, offering the precious egg to the girl in the indigo shawl. The man scowled and shuffled away.

As the girl's lips moved, Luke again offered her the sugar shell. A slight frown turned down the corners of her mouth, and a question came to her eyes. But the boy persisted. He put the egg into her hands. Then, pointing to the light, he raised her hands to her eyes.

Bewildered, the girl looked inside the egg. When her back stiffened, Luke knew she had understood: a dusty road winding past Gordon's pond. Beyond the pond lay a red barn and a white farmhouse with a smoking chimney. On the chimney, a row of bricks was painted white. This was the secret sign.

Here was a painting of the new safe haven—Price's farm.

The girl lowered the egg and cradled it in her own hands. Glancing at the man, she took a coin from her purse and pressed it into Luke's hand. She held it there for a moment. *You have done what needed doing,* her eyes told him. Then with a nod, she swept out the door.

Luke's eyes followed her outside and watched as she clambered aboard the buggy. Was the man watching, too? The boy turned his eyes to a waiting customer, but his thoughts remained beyond the door.

If he could lay his hand on the floorboard of that buggy, would he feel the heartbeat of someone hiding underneath, and would that someone feel his own heart quake?

As the buggy lurched forward, Luke placed another sugar egg into the cupped hands of an eager child.

LOOK TOWARD THE LIGHT, Luke signed. LOOK TOWARD THE LIGHT.

AFTERWORD

When the Civil War began in 1861, The American School for the Deaf had already been operating in Hartford, Connecticut, for forty-five years. It was one of twenty-four schools for deaf children in the United States at that time. Students learned to read, write, and communicate in speech and sign language.

Signs of a different sort were used along the Underground Railroad. In Vermont, some say, a row of chimney bricks painted white signaled a safe house or "station." Between 1800 and 1860, thousands of men, women, and children found their way to freedom with the help of people like Luke, Mama, and the girl in the indigo shawl.

Although much remains unknown about the Underground Railroad, one thing is certain: the Fugitive Slave Law of 1793 made it a crime to assist an escaped slave. Slave catchers were permitted to seize runaways—even in free states—and received monetary rewards for their efforts. Officers of the law were obliged to help these bounty hunters until slaves in the Confederate States were finally declared free on January 1, 1863—when President Lincoln issued the Emancipation Proclamation.